The Northern Woods Adventure

Early Reader

Written and Illustrated by Gary Harbo

Published by KUTIE KARI BOOKS, INC.
Printed in the United States of America

The Northern Woods Adventure

Early Reader

ISBN 1-884149-16-2

To order books visit Gary's website:
www.garyharbo.com

In Memory of My Father

I dedicate this book to my father, who taught me how to be a child.
How to explore and question everything, and that it was okay to be a little wild.

As hard as he worked in life, he took the time to bring us up to the North Shore.
As we traveled all across Minnesota, he taught me how much I had to be thankful for.

We traveled to Bemidji and Park Rapids, and saw where the mighty Mississippi was born.
He taught me the wonders of nature, and how much beauty there was in a farmer's field of corn.

We would sit and talk for hours, with our bobbers floating lazily on a big blue lake.
I never really cared if I caught a fish; it was the warmth of his attention that I loved to take.

He taught me how to talk to people, and to listen respectfully to what they had to say.
For I would never learn anything new, if I only listened to myself all day.

He taught me that everybody makes them, but that I had to learn from my mistakes.
And no matter how hard it seems to fix them, I needed to do whatever it would take.

He taught me about truth and honor, and how important it is to keep your word.
As I look back in life I realize, these golden truths I was lucky to have heard.

As I created this book I realized, that he was constantly on my mind.
For learning life's lessons, a better teacher I would never find.

Thank you LORD,
         for placing him in my life...

Merle Antone Harbo
December 19, 1933 - August 1, 1986

Grannie Jannie told Bart, Kari, Herby and the gang that they were going on a vacation across northern Minnesota, and they were so excited by the news.

When Grannie introduced Babbaran to the friends,

Bart's eyes bugged out in delight, but she wasn't in the least bit amused.

Mall of America

1

They visited the Walker Art Center
and had a very nice lunch.

But when Bart tried to flirt with
Babbaran,

she blasted him with her water soaker
and he fell with a crunch.

Minneapolis skyline

4

Grannie got them all into the R.V. and headed up north to Potato Lake.

Bart wanted to try water skiing,

but he would soon find out that it would be an awefully big mistake.

Potato Lake

5

Bart was showing off as the boat
began a big turn to the right.

When he gave the girls a peace sign,

his skis crossed, the rope gave a jerk
and boy was he ever a sight.

Then it was on to the mouth of the Mississippi in Itasca State Park.

Bart raced after a funny little frog named Eddie,

who seemed just as happy as a lark.

Itasca State Park

HERE 1475 FT
ABOVE
THE OCEAN
THE MIGHTY
MISSISSIPPI
BEGINS
TO FLOW
ON ITS
WINDING WAY
2552 MILES
TO THE
GULF
OF MEXICO

Bart had fun chasing Eddie,
and they became good friends.

After arriving in Bemidji,

Bart flexed his muscles for Babbaran,
but she rolled her eyes once again.

Bemidji

When they arrived in Brainerd, they
decided to go jet skiing on Gull Lake.

Bart tried to do a wild 360,

but Eddie was launched
like a rocket for goodness sake.

Gull Lake

13

15

The next day they drove through Duluth
and made it to Gooseberry Falls.

As they explored the gorgeous river,

Bart slipped on the rocks
and gave out a deafening call.

Gooseberry Falls State Park

At daybreak they made it to Split Rock lighthouse to take in the beautiful sunrise.

As Kari was watching a huge cargo ship,

Brandon was taking a picture of Slimey who was posing for the camera, which should come as no surprise.

Split Rock Lighthouse

17

18

When they reached Tettegouche State Park, they put their canoes in the Baptism River.

Everyone was so busy fishing,

they didn't notice that Eddie and Bart were drifting towards a huge waterfall that would make even a grown-up quiver.

High Falls

Bart was bolted out of sleep by a
mosquito that had just finished its bite.

Then Eddie noticed that
they had lost their paddle,

and he could hear Two Step Falls
and the thunder of all its might.

Tettegouche State Park

21

Herby and Kari noticed that Bart was gone,
so they all raced ahead of the canoe.

When they pulled down a tree,

and Babbaran grabbed his hand,
Bart thought it was pretty cool.

Two Step Falls

After that awesome rescue,
it was on to Lake Kabetogama,
and everyone was without a care.

But while they were roasting
their marshmallows,

Bart was behind the bushes
pretending to growl like a bear.

Voyageurs National Park

What Bart didn't seem to realize,
is that a bear was really in the brush.

When he turned to see
what was behind him,

the bear was ready to strike Bart
with one powerful crush.

As everyone raced for the cabin, Eddie decided that he had to help his friend.

So he leaped onto the bear's nose,

and grabbed him by the ears hoping he could hang on until the end.

When the bear got tired of shaking him,
it gave up and finally walked away.

Bart raced over to Eddie and told him,

"Little buddy, you saved the day!"

THE END

Gary Harbo was raised in Lynd, a farming community in southwestern Minnesota. This quiet little town of 200 people was a great place to grow up in and learn about life. Gary loved playing baseball, basketball and football, as well as reading and drawing. When Gary was 9 years old, his parents began to save his drawings and encouraged him to pursue his talent. To this day he hasn't forgotten how great it felt to have his drawings hanging from his parents walls. His love of drawing resulted in several first place finishes in art competitions for his wildlife colored-pencil illustrations.

All through life Gary has been successful because he has been blessed with a great imagination and a wonderful ability to look at life through the eyes of a child. In 1990 he created cartoon characters that were loaded with personality. His children, Kari and Gary II, were at the root of this inspiration. In 1991, at the age of 33, Gary left the corporate world and jumped head-first into the magical world of children's books. Since then, Gary and his wife Barb have added two cute little boys named Grant and Gavin. Gary has used all of this motivation to write and illustrate six humorous picture books, **My New Friend**, **Bad Bart's Revenge**, **Bart Becomes a Friend**, **The Great Train Ride**, **The Black Hills Adventure**, and **The Northern Woods Adventure**. These action-packed adventures are bringing smiles to hundreds of thousands of children across the Midwest.

As an author and illustrator, Gary teaches art lessons to over 25,000 elementary school children every year. His motivational talks encompass the whole process of writing, illustrating and publishing. His talks include; Keynote Speaker for the International Reading Association Conventions, Chapter One Parent/Children workshops, Guest Author for Young Authors Conferences, as well as Author-in-Residences for hundreds of schools in many states.

For information on how to get Gary to share his talents at your school, call 651-450-7427 or e-mail gharbo@garyharbo.com. Gary also does free art lessons every month on his web site: www.garyharbo.com so check it out.

Bart and his Circle of Friends